LENA'S STORY

Bloomsbury Education
An imprint of Bloomsbury Publishing Plc

50 Bedford Square
London
WC1B 3DP
UK

1385 Broadway
New York
NY 10018
USA

www.bloomsbury.com

BLOOMSBURY and the Diana logo are trademarks of Bloomsbury Publishing Plc

First published in 2017 by Bloomsbury Education

ISBN
PB: 978-1-4729-3400-0
ePub: 978-1-4729-3401-7
ePDF: 978-1-4729-3398-0

2 4 6 8 10 9 7 5 3 1

Printed in China by Leo Paper Products

MIX
Paper from
responsible sources
FSC® C020056

This book is produced using paper that is made from wood grown in managed,
sustainable forests. It is natural, renewable and recyclable. The logging and manufacturing
processes conform to the environmental regulations of the country of origin.

To find out more about our authors and books visit www.bloomsbury.com.
Here you will find extracts, author interviews, details of forthcoming
events and the option to sign up for our newsletters.

recommended by

www.catchup.org

Catch Up is a charity which aims to address the problem of underachievement that
has its roots in literacy and numeracy difficulties.

JUDY WAITE

LENA'S STORY

Illustrated by Chris Askham

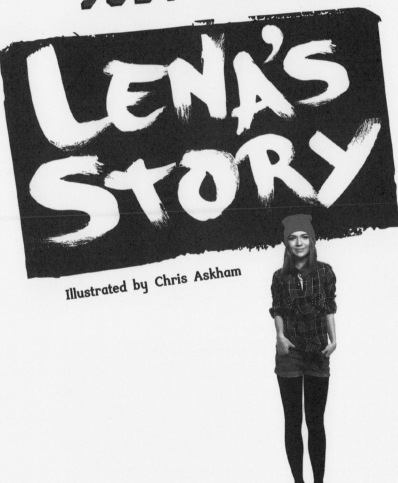

BLOOMSBURY EDUCATION
AN IMPRINT OF BLOOMSBURY

LONDON OXFORD NEW YORK NEW DELHI SYDNEY

THE STREET

Lena, Kai, Sanjay and Chelsea live on Swatton High Street.

They are fourteen years old, and they are best friends. They'll never let each other down...

CONTENTS

Chapter One
Hit and Run

Lena and Chelsea were out on Swatton High Street. Suddenly Lena grabbed Chelsea's arm.

"There's a puppy in the road!" she cried, and pointed to a brown puppy that was racing along the street. "It might get hit by a car if we don't catch it. It could be killed."

Chelsea was dropping coins into a charity collection tin for injured soldiers. The collector had been in the army with her brother, Tommy. She turned to where Lena was pointing. "It's just racing up and down. I can't bear to look," she said nervously.

Their friends Sanjay and Kai ran up behind them.

"What's up?" asked Kai. He looked at Lena in the way that always made her heart beat faster.

Lena was glad he couldn't see the effect he had on her. She turned her attention back to the puppy. "Look at that puppy. We need to do something. He could get killed!" she cried.

"It looks a bit crazy," said Sanjay. He put two fingers in his mouth and whistled, but the puppy didn't take any notice. It was chasing an empty drink can. It barked wildly as the can rolled towards the gutter. A car blasted its horn and swerved.

"It can't hear that whistle. Not with all this traffic noise," said Chelsea. "Maybe we should…"

But Lena didn't stop to listen to Chelsea's suggestion. She ran to the traffic lights and pressed the button for the crossing. The cars stopped and she stepped into the road. "Here boy, come here," she called. "Come to me."

The puppy wagged his tail but ran off down the street. At the same moment, Chelsea screamed. "Lena, look behind you!"

Kai and Sanjay were yelling too.

"Watch out!"

"You're gonna get hit!"

Lena turned.

Two cyclists were hurtling towards her, overtaking the waiting cars. They were both wearing helmets that hid their faces. Lena could hear the one in front shouting, "Get out of the way!"

Lena felt frozen with fear. They were coming straight at her.

Kai and Sanjay were still yelling. Their shouts broke Lena's trance. She leapt sideways just as the bikes raced past. "Idiots!" she called after them. Her legs felt weak as Kai grabbed her. He pulled her back to the pavement.

Suddenly there was another yell. The four friends turned in horror. The puppy was dodging to get away from the first bike, and was right in the path of the second one. The second bike clipped the back leg of the puppy, knocking him backwards. His terrified yelps filled the air.

"NO!" screamed Lena.

The bikes raced away. They hadn't even tried to swerve.

Chapter Two
The Blame Game

Lena clutched the puppy tightly as she ran home. Chelsea, Kai and Sanjay ran with her. They burst in through the front door.

"What's all the fuss?" Lena's dad appeared in the hallway. "I'm having a meeting with my new boss in the kitchen. We don't need all this noise," he said.

"This puppy got hit by a bike," Lena explained, and she relaxed her hold on the puppy to let Dad have a look. The puppy wriggled and jumped from her arms.

"Hmmph, he doesn't look hurt," grumbled Dad.

"Yay! I think he's OK," said Sanjay, grinning as the puppy sniffed at a briefcase by the stairs. Then the puppy scampered up to a pot plant and began chewing the leaves.

"No bones broken then," added Kai. "He's bounding from one thing to another. Awesome."

Lena smiled at him. Trust Kai to be impressed by something 'bounding'. Earlier that day she'd watched Kai train for kick-boxing and he was pretty good at bounding himself. Jumping, spinning and kicking. Watching him had given her another one of those 'heart–beat' moments, but she'd pushed it away. First, he lived next door. And second, there were always girls begging for his attention. Dating the boy next door was way too obvious. Anyhow, she was never going to beg for attention from any guy.

She turned to the puppy again. "Dad, he's so cute. Can I keep him?" Lena suddenly wanted this puppy more than anything. He'd felt so warm when she held him, and she had never had a pet. Dad always said they couldn't afford it, but he had regular work now. Things were better than when they'd first arrived from Poland. She'd only been six then – it was eight years ago – but she still remembered how bad it had been.

"No." Dad shook his head. "It takes a lot of time to look after a dog. You would be better off getting a Saturday job and earning some money. Your mum said they're advertising in The Street Café."

Lena pouted. Waitressing on a Saturday was not on her list of things to do.

"I **have** got time for a dog," she said. "Now that the theatre has closed and I don't have drama lessons any more, I can take him out for walks." Lena pouted again. She could usually get round Dad. "I've got a **huge** hole in my life that needs filling. And it won't be filled by carrying coffee cups to strangers."

She felt her eyes sting with tears, and she didn't wipe them away. It was good for Dad to see how much this mattered.

Dad looked from Lena to the puppy, and she could see he was thinking about the idea. "We'll talk about it later, when Mum finishes her shift at the hospital," he said.

Sanjay was still trying to catch the puppy, but the puppy scampered away into the kitchen.

"Please, Dad..."

At that moment there was a shout from the kitchen. "No! No! Let go!" There was a yelp and the puppy shot back into the hall again. Dad, Lena and her friends rushed to see what had happened.

Dad's boss, Mr Bukoski, was standing by the kitchen table. He held out one arm for them all to see. "That dog jumped up and tore my sleeve. This is a new jacket." Mr Bukoski looked furious.

"I'm so sorry," Dad looked furious too. He turned to Lena's friends. "It's time for you to leave. And take that... **animal** with you."

"I'll catch him," said Chelsea.

Lena watched her friends hurry away. They called goodbye as they left the house.

Lena knew there would be no chance of her keeping the puppy now. But what would happen to him? Sanjay couldn't keep him in his family's Curry House restaurant. Chelsea's mum ran The Crown pub, and wouldn't even let dogs in the garden. Kai's mum had a new baby. None of them would cope with a pet.

"Make Mr Bukoski a coffee. Strong and black, the way he likes it," said Dad. "We all need to sit down and calm down."

Mr Bukoski shook his head. "I don't want coffee." He still sounded angry. "I have other workers to talk to. I'll be in touch if I need you," he said, turning to Dad.

"I'll show you out." Dad gave Lena another angry look. She felt sick. If Dad lost this work because of her, then they would be poor again. Mum would have to do extra shifts. Her parents would be tired and stressed all the time.

Dad led Mr Bukoski into the hall. She heard them talking by the front door. A moment later, there was a shout.

Dad strode back into the kitchen. "One of your friends has taken Mr Bukoski's wallet. It is not in his briefcase. You had better find out which one of them did it or he will tell the police."

Chapter Three
Runaway

Lena slammed out of the house. She was very angry. She raced past the kebab shop and then crossed the street by The Crown pub. Chelsea's mum was cleaning the windows.

Chelsea's mum waved, but Lena was too upset to wave back. She didn't want to speak to anyone. Most of all she couldn't face seeing her friends. There was no way she was going to tell them that Dad and his boss thought they were thieves. How dare Dad say that about them! Stupid Mr Bukoski. He probably lost his wallet before he even got to their house.

She slowed down once she was past The Curry House and stopped as she got near to the old Jester theatre. It was so sad to see it boarded up. She'd been in loads of shows there.

Dad said the drama club was worth paying out for. Lena had heard him tell a workmate that learning lines was a good way to practise her English. Dad said speaking good English was important for the future, but she had not been given many lines to learn. Once she was cast as a squawking penguin. Dad was **not** impressed. He thought it was a waste of time. Lena scowled at the thought of Dad. She hoped he wouldn't come looking for her.

She turned down the road that led to the back of the theatre. It was boarded up round there too. There was a 'KEEP OUT' sign on the back door.

The building was probably dangerous. The walls might crumble. The roof might fall in.

Lena didn't care. She needed somewhere to shelter. She was never going home again, not now Dad had been so horrible about her friends. And if he did lose his job because of her, she'd be in endless trouble anyway.

Lena pushed at the door. It opened easily. Too easily. Almost as if someone had been there before her. But still Lena didn't care. It was probably some homeless people hanging out there at night. She knew the theatre really well. There were plenty of places she could hide. No one would find her.

Chapter Four
Man in the Mirror

The theatre was dusty and dark. Lena crept past the props room and along the corridor. She went past the rows of faded velvet seats that faced the stage. She had sat there lots of times, sometimes watching the rest of her drama club rehearse, sometimes just being in the audience. She kept moving, going towards the dressing rooms. Lena knew her way around. She could have walked it blindfolded. She felt a thrill as she reached the first dressing room. This was the star's room. She'd never been in it before. She turned the door handle. The door opened with a creak.

The dressing room was dark but a pale sun shone through the dirty window. Its rays were reflected in the cracked mirror.

Lena could see shabby costumes hanging from a rail. She went over and touched them. There were dresses and cloaks, and a row of old soldiers' uniforms. "I remember these uniforms," she murmured to herself. "They were worn in a play I saw with my school. It was about the First World War."

She remembered more of her own costumes. One year, she'd been a fairy. She'd had to creep up a narrow, secret staircase behind the stage with all the other fairies. They had fluttered around the balcony seats, and all the mums and dads had said how cute they looked.

Her own dad had thought that too. Now, he was thinking she hung around with a bunch of criminals.

A movement in the mirror caught her eye. Lena got a glimpse of a pale, thin figure dressed in a soldier's uniform. She spun around to check, but there was no one there. Her heart thudded as she turned back to the mirror. The reflection was gone.

Lena frowned. Did the theatre have a ghost lurking about?

She moved away, stepping over a scattering of old shoes that lay on the floor.

Suddenly, one of the shoes moved on its own.

Lena screamed.

Chapter Five
Haunted

Lena watched, horrified, as the moving shoe scrambled onto a pile of old curtains. The shoe had a long, thin tail.

A rat! Lena wasn't sure if rats were worse than ghosts, but she wasn't going to hang about any longer.

She ran back out towards the seats.

This was her 'happy place'. Nothing bad would happen here. She could still remember the way the theatre had been when it was packed. Upstairs the balcony area was in shadow, but she remembered sitting there with Chelsea on the school trip. It had been great sitting up so high. She'd felt a bit dizzy too. They had both freaked out, imagining what it would be like to fall over the safety railings.

Lena looked up at the domed ceiling. There were a few cracks in the gold patterns, but it all looked solid.

Lena didn't think it was about to fall down onto her head. She liked being out by the stage, with space around her. There wasn't really a ghost in the dressing room. It was probably just one of the costumes reflected in the mirror. As for the rat – well, so what? Rats had to live somewhere, and they liked corners they could tuck into. It wouldn't come after her out here.

She sat in the front row, in one of the faded velvet seats. "I danced here once, on that stage," she said out loud. "People watched me. People clapped."

Her voice echoed through the empty theatre. Lena looked at the stage that no one would ever dance on again.

Then the idea came to her.

She would dance on it one last time.

She would sing too. Maybe the rats would even come out to watch.

She giggled as she stood up. "Ladies and gentlemen, my name is Lena Kowlaski, the star of this show. I promise you singing, dancing and absolutely no squawking penguins. Not even the squeak of one."

She walked towards the stage, still smiling. But then the smile froze on her face. Someone was already there. He was watching her.

His face was pale and thin.

He wore a soldier's uniform.

"I'm so glad you've decided to join me up here," he said. His voice was whispery. Half words, half moan. "I've been so lonely, for sooo long."

Lena gave a moan of her own, only hers was a moan of true terror.

Chapter Six
Ghostly Army

Lena ran down the aisle. She turned to look, terrified that the ghost would be behind her, about to grab her.

But he was still on the stage. Still watching her.

Lena was shaking so hard that her teeth chattered.

She wanted to get home. She would get that job in The Street Café and pay Mr Bukoski whatever he wanted. She would learn dressmaking and fix his jacket. She would be a perfect daughter who never did anything wrong.

She raced along the corridor, stumbling past the props room. An old mop loomed like a sneering witch. Something fluttered up to the ceiling.

She could hear small, desperate sobs echoing around her – and then realised the sobs were hers. "Please, let me get out. Let me get out."

But as she reached the back door, the ghost appeared in front of her. It stood swaying, pale and terrible. "Hello, lovely Lena. I hope you're not leaving. I'm still waiting to see your show."

"H–how did you get here?" Lena backed away from the door, crashing into the mop. It clattered onto the floor.

"Lena... Lena." The ghost's voice was still whispery. It seemed to drift around her like smoke. Lena felt as if everything were spinning. She felt giddy with fear. There were other voices now, all calling her name.

"Lena."

"Lena."

How many ghosts were there? Ten? A hundred? Her mind was full of the ghosts. Lena stumbled backwards over the fallen mop and fell to the floor.

Chapter Seven
Stare Scare

A ghost was attacking Lena. It was chewing her arm and licking her face. Even though Lena was still dazed from the fall, she knew the idea of a chewing, licking ghost was crazy.

She opened her eyes. Chelsea, Kai and Sanjay all stared down at her.

The puppy bounced around her and licked her face again.

"You?" Lena sat up slowly, rubbing her eyes. "I thought it was a ghost." She tried to push the puppy away. "Hey, you. I'm not a tasty snack," she said.

She turned back to her friends. "How did you know I was here?"

"Your dad rang my mum," said Chelsea.

"He said you'd run off because of a misunderstanding. He was worried about you.

Mum had seen you heading this way, so she texted me. She said you looked upset."

"Oh, yeah." Lena felt herself blush as she remembered what Dad had said about her friends. She hoped he hadn't told them about the missing wallet.

Sanjay helped Lena to her feet. Kai picked the puppy up and put him to one side. The puppy jumped up on his hind legs and stuck his nose in Kai's back pocket. "Hey, get off my bum," Kai laughed. "Look, he's nicked my house-key this time."

"He keeps taking stuff," Chelsea said. "Then he runs off and buries it. We've called him Robbie. Robbie the robber-dog."

They all watched as Robbie tried to bury Kai's keys under a pile of old theatre programmes.

Lena rested her head on Kai's shoulder. "It's so good to see you all," she sighed.

"It's good to see you too," said Chelsea. She hugged Lena.

"But what was it you were saying about a ghost?" asked Sanjay. "When we turned up we only saw you, just tangled up with a mop on the floor."

"Come with me." Lena led them through towards the stage. It was empty.

"I must have imagined it," Lena shrugged. "It felt weird being here on my own, and I was upset about some – er – stuff with my dad. I think my head must have got a bit screwed up."

Chelsea looked round. "There's nothing here. Just dust and cobwebs. Probably a few pigeons in that broken roof."

Suddenly, Robbie began to bark.

Lena picked him up but he wriggled free and ran under a row of seats. "He must be scared," she said.

"Him and me both," said Sanjay. "Look what's sitting in the front row, staring at an empty stage."

Chelsea gave a small shriek. "It looks like a ghost! The ghost of a soldier."

Chapter Eight
Threat

Lena felt braver with the others there. "Let's go nearer," she murmured. "Perhaps we can help him. Maybe his spirit is trapped in time, and he doesn't know how to leave."

She walked slowly down the aisle.

The ghost turned, and gave her his thin smile. "So you came back. And you brought your own audience this time."

"We want to help you," Lena said. "We think your soul might be trapped."

The ghost laughed. It was a proper laugh – not thin and whispery – but it still wasn't a kind laugh. "I'm sure you can help me," he said. "How about you pay me to leave?"

"Pay you?" Kai had been close behind Lena and he walked round to stand by her side. "Are you saying that ghosts need money in ghost-world?"

Chelsea and Sanjay joined them. Lena noticed they were standing close together. She felt a rush of warmth for her friends. They were all scared, but none of them would let her face this ghost on her own.

The ghost stood up. "Yeah, that's right," he said. "We spirits need to pay our way in the afterlife, just like anyone else."

"You don't sound much like a ghost," said Sanjay.

"Woooo oooooo," said the ghost, and gave a little jump towards them. Chelsea squealed and Sanjay stepped backwards, but neither of them ran away.

"You still don't sound like a ghost," said Sanjay.

"More like an owl," added Chelsea, although Lena could hear her voice was shaky.

"But he must be a ghost. He was on stage, and then he was at the door before I got there," said Lena, and she shook her head. "There's no way a real person could have got ahead of me..."

Kai interrupted. "I don't know how he tricked you, but this isn't a ghost." He reached forward and poked the ghost in the chest. "Look: solid. Alive."

Lena's eyes widened. Kai was right. "You're wearing a costume from the dressing room. The ones they wore in the First World War play."

The ghost stepped back. "Well done. We could say you've seen through me. Ha ha."

"Very funny," muttered Sanjay. "You're just a human. Probably only a few years older than us."

"Real flesh and blood." The boy pulled out a knife. "If you cut me, I'd bleed."

Chelsea gasped.

"Put that away." Lena tried to keep her voice level. The blade looked long, and sharp.

The boy waved the knife at her. "I was planning on collecting cash for my own... er... charity," he said. "This old army costume was perfect for the part. Now I can save myself the trouble. Just give me whatever money you've got and I'll go."

"You're joking." Kai suddenly seemed to take control. He reached forward again. The boy stepped sideways, but his heavy soldier's boot got caught in a loose floorboard. He stumbled, and the knife fell to the floor.

He tried to grab it, but Kai moved faster. Kai held the knife.

"No," Lena's voice shook. "Kai, don't do anything stupid."

"Yeah, keep calm," said Sanjay. "Why don't we just all leave?"

"Maybe you should." The boy gave his thin, cruel smile. "But you might have to leave something behind." He pointed upwards, towards the balcony seats.

Lena and the others all looked at where he was pointing.

A thin, pale figure in another soldier's uniform was sitting in the front row. It got up slowly, and leant over the safety railings. Something small and brown wriggled in its arms. The figure spoke. "If you want to see this stupid mutt again, then I suggest you give my brother the cash he's asking for."

Chelsea's voice trembled as she spoke. "He must be a twin... and he's going to throw Robbie off the balcony."

Chapter Nine
Take Two

Sanjay turned back to the first twin. "We don't want any trouble," he said.

"None of us should be here," Kai added. "The security guards will show up if we don't leave now."

"That's right." Chelsea joined in. "Lena's dad is looking for her, and my mum knows we came here. Either of them might turn up, too."

"We can make a quick getaway if we have to," the boy sneered. "Me and Perry have got our bikes outside. We can be gone in a shot."

Lena gasped. These must be the two who had ridden their bikes at Robbie. They wouldn't care at all about dropping him. They probably hurt animals for fun.

She looked up at the twin on the balcony.

It was a mega-drop to the ground. There was no way the puppy would survive the fall. She could hear Robbie's little puppy yelps and could see him wagging his tail. He was probably thinking this was some new sort of game. She remembered how much she'd wished he was hers.

"Keep soldier-boy talking," she whispered to Chelsea. "Try and make him think you might give him some money."

"I haven't got any," Chelsea whispered back.

"Just pretend. I know you'll think of something," muttered Lena.

"Why? What are you going to do?" Chelsea whispered again.

"I've got an idea." Lena squeezed her friend's arm. "Just trust me." She edged away.

Chelsea stepped forward, holding her phone up. "You can have this," she said. "There's a second-hand shop along the street. They buy phones there."

Lena saw the twins exchange glances. She wondered if they could read each other's minds. Chelsea had done well. Now Lena could sneak off.

She crept away, then darted down the corridor that led around to the backstage area.

In front of her was a narrow wooden door. It was the door to the secret stairs – the ones she'd tiptoed up when she was a fairy.

The area was sound-proofed. She couldn't hear the others any more. If she couldn't hear them, they wouldn't hear her.

The door was stiff. Or locked. She pushed at the wood panels. They creaked, but didn't break. She suddenly remembered Kai with his kick-boxing. The way he jumped and spun and kicked. He'd told her that whenever he had a fight looming, he'd imagine himself doing all the moves. Being fast. Being awesome.

Lena had laughed at him then, but it didn't seem funny any more. She closed her eyes. She imagined herself jumping. Spinning. Kicking.

Then, with a wild leap, she jumped, span around, and swung a kick towards the door.

It broke easily, one side panel splitting away. At the same moment a blood-curdling yowl filled the air.

Chapter Ten
Into the Dark

Lena stood, terrified. What was happening?

She wanted to go back, but then she thought about Robbie. There was no way she was going to give up trying to save him.

Taking a deep breath, she edged through the gap in the door. At the same moment a scrawny ginger cat yowled again. It rushed away up the stairs, its tail held high.

Lena almost laughed. A cat!

"Sorry, Mr Cat," she called softly. "I'm not chasing you. But I've got to come up these stairs too."

She rushed up the stairs and slowed down as she reached the top. Then she took a deep breath. She crept out onto the back of the balcony. It was dark and full of shadows.

Chapter Eleven
End Game

Perry was still standing between the front row and the railings. He was still holding Robbie.

Lena crept between the rows of seats. She had to keep low. If the first twin saw she was creeping up on his brother, it would be game over for poor Robbie. And if he got the knife back from Kai, it might be game over for her friends too.

Chelsea was clutching her phone. "Your brother has to let Robbie go, before I give you this," she said.

"No chance." The first twin sneered. "Why should we trust you?"

"You are the ones who seem happy to splatter a puppy over the floor," said Kai. "We would be stupid to take chances with you."

"One phone isn't enough," Perry shouted down to them. "Me and Preston want cash as well." He held Robbie high and rocked his body slightly, as if he was getting ready to throw.

"This phone is all I've got," begged Chelsea. "Please."

Sanjay turned his pockets out. "Look. Empty. I haven't got cash either."

"I've got coins. Four quid. Have it." Kai threw his money onto the floor.

Lena was crouching three rows from the front. Perry held Robbie high. She would have to do something quickly – except she had no idea what that 'something' might be.

She crept along between the front two rows. She could see through the gaps between the seats and the safety railings.

She couldn't see everything that was going on, but she could see enough.

Preston stooped to pick up the coins, keeping one eye on the knife in Kai's hand.

"If there's no more cash, then we want all your phones," he said. "Put them on the floor and slide them towards me." Chelsea, Kai and Sanjay dropped their phones on the floor. Lena was relieved. If the twins accepted the phones, then she might not need to do anything.

Preston went to pick up the phones, but then stopped. "Hey, hang on a minute. There should be four of you. Where's the lovely Miss Lena Kowlaski?"

Lena saw Perry begin to turn, moving back from the railings. There was no time left. Whatever she was going to do, she had to do it now.

Then two things happened at once. Lena scrambled over the front row seat and grabbed Perry by the shoulders. She pushed him sideways.

At the same time, there was a bark and a yelp. Robbie had spotted the cat. He leapt away from Perry and chased the cat up between the seats, and out through an upstairs exit.

"Robbie's got away," Lena yelled. "These twins can't threaten us any more."

"You don't think so?" said Perry, and he grabbed at Lena.

He was stronger than her. He stood up and pulled her with him. He was gripping her shoulders. Pushing Lena forwards, he grinned at Preston down below.

Kai, Sanjay and Chelsea all stared with new horror.

Lena knew what they were thinking. How crazy were these twins? Was Perry mad enough to throw **her** over the balcony?

Chapter Twelve
Curtain Call

Preston glared up at Perry. "You're an idiot," he shouted. "You can't even keep hold of a stupid puppy."

Perry stopped grinning. "Lena surprised me. She knocked me over," he whined.

"That's even worse. She's much smaller than you!" Preston seemed to have forgotten about the phones. He seemed to be fed up with Perry.

Kai still held the knife.

Chelsea shouted up at Perry. "You do anything to Lena and we'll do something to your brother." But Lena could hear her friend's voice shaking. The twins would know she was bluffing. There was no way Kai would use the knife. He was just playing for time. But time for what? Perry had something to prove now. He only had to push her hard. Lena didn't imagine she'd flutter like a fairy. The drop would be fast, ugly, and final.

It was Sanjay who made things happen.

Darting forward, he grabbed his phone back, punching in numbers. "Police. We need help. There's a guy attacking my friend at the Jester theatre, on the corner of Swatton High Street." He waved his phone at Preston. "The cops are pretty quick around here. How do you fancy life behind bars?" he asked.

Preston scowled at him. "Get stuffed," he said. But he started backing away, and then turned and ran.

Perry was still gripping Lena. "Hey," he called after Preston. "What do you want me to do?"

Lena took a deep breath. "He wants you to follow him," she said. "I know twins always do everything together."

"She's right," Kai shouted up. "Plus, if the police catch you and not him, he'll be even more fed up with you."

Perry hesitated. Then he shoved Lena backwards, scrambled over the seats and made his own escape.

At the same time Robbie bounded back in, wagging his tail. He had a crumpled theatre poster in his mouth. He dropped it at Lena's feet. Lena bent to stroke the puppy's ears.

She buried her face in his soft fur and he wriggled, trying to chew her ear.

"You OK?" Looking up, she saw Kai running down the aisle towards her.

"Yeah. Just about," she said, with a shaky smile.

Kai put his arms around her and hugged her. Lena's heart thumped wildly, but this time it was with relief. Relief that Robbie was safe, and relief that she had such awesome friends.

"Do we have to wait for the police now?" she said. "Will we have to give statements?"

Sanjay and Chelsea came down the aisle too. Sanjay shook his head. "My battery was flat. I didn't make the call. I was acting," he grinned, but he looked shaky too.

Lena lifted her head from Kai's shoulder, looking towards the stage. "Seems we have all just given the performances of our lives. I hope those two get picked up for something else. They deserve to be caught."

"I'm sure they will be caught for something soon," said Chelsea. "They are trouble."

Lena nodded. "Double trouble," she said.

Above them, something creaked. They all looked up. A pigeon fluttered through a crack in the ceiling. "We must get out before the roof falls in on us," said Sanjay. "I suggest we take a final bow, then run for it."

Chapter Thirteen
Puppy Love

Lena burst in through her front door, carrying Robbie.

"Dad!" She raced into the kitchen. "We need to talk. I think I know what happened to Mr Bukoski's wallet."

"Shhh – no need to shout," said Mum. She was sitting at the table, drinking coffee. "Oh, hello, puppy!" Mum made a clucking noise with her mouth. Robbie wriggled out of Lena's arms and bounded over to her.

Moments later Mum was kneeling on the floor with Robbie, tickling his tummy.

Dad looked up from checking his emails on his laptop. "You don't need to explain anything, Lena," he said. "The wallet turned up half buried in the plant-pot by the front door. I'm sorry I suspected your friends. I feel very ashamed."

"I knew it would be something like that,"
Lena said. "This afternoon Robbie stole Kai's
keys and tried to bury them. And later he
snatched Chelsea's phone and..." She hesitated.
She wasn't sure it was a good idea to admit
that a knife had been pulled on them inside
a crumbling theatre. "Anyway, he's just a
naughty puppy, but in a super-cute way.
So, Dad, if I take that Saturday job at the café
and earn enough to buy all Robbie's food, can
I keep him? Please?"

Dad and Mum exchanged glances.

Robbie jumped up, grabbed an oven glove from the kitchen worktop, and bounded out to the hall with it.

"You can see how naughty he is," Lena begged. "I'll have to train him. I'll need to learn all sorts of skills. Maybe one day I'll be a police-dog trainer."

Suddenly Dad looked interested.

Mum hid her smile behind her hand.

"Yes," sighed Dad. "It's my way of offering my biggest apology."

Lena hugged Dad. "Apology accepted," she grinned.

She ran out into the hallway, where Robbie was busy burying the oven glove underneath the 'Welcome' mat beside the front door.

Bonus Bits!

Quiz Time!

Check how well you paid attention to the story by answering these multiple choice questions. The answers are at the end of this section – no peeping!

1 What was the puppy chasing at the start of the story?

   a a ball

   b a chip paper

   c an empty drink can

   d a page of a newspaper

2 How did Sanjay try and get the puppy's attention when it was running in the road?

a he whistled

b he shouted

c he called

d he threw a stick

3 Which country had Lena lived in until she was six years old?

a Brazil

b Poland

c Sweden

d France

4 Why was Mr Bukoski so cross when he was in the kitchen?

a he had spilled his cup of coffee

b his wallet had been stolen

c Lena's dad did not agree to the deal

d the puppy had torn the sleeve of his jacket

5 Why did Lena go into the theatre?

a she wanted somewhere to shelter

b she had a drama class

c she wanted to find a disguise

d she had agreed to meet her friends there

6 What did Lena see in the mirror?

   a a ginger cat

   b her dad

   c a thin, pale figure dressed in a soldier's uniform

   d the missing puppy

7 What made the shoe 'move on its own'?

   a a ghost

   b a rat

   c the wind

   d a cat

8 What did the puppy take from Kai's pocket?

   a his house-key

   b a dog treat

   c his wallet

   d a sandwich

9 What does the 'ghost' say they can do to help him?

a play a game with him

b give him some food

c pay him to leave

d help him find the exit

10 Why does Lena know the boys won't care about hurting the puppy?

a they have their own dog

b they have hurt other dogs

c they had threatened the children with a knife

d they had already hurt him when they were on their bikes

11 What is the name of the twin who had the knife?

a Perry

b Robbie

c Preston

d Peter

12 What made the twin who had had the knife turn and run?

a Sanjay said he had called the police

b Sanjay had threatened him with the knife

What Next?

Have a think about these questions after reading this story:

- The twins were planning to pretend to be soldiers and ask people for money – what is wrong with this?
- Why is it dangerous to carry a knife around? What could have happened and how would this have changed the lives of those involved?
- How do you think the children felt during the time they were in the theatre with the twins?

ANSWERS to QUIZ TIME!

1c, 2a, 3b, 4d, 5a, 6c, 7b, 8a, 9c, 10d, 11c, 12a

If you enjoyed reading this story, look out for *Kai's Story: Going Viral*. Find it, curl up somewhere and READ IT!